This book belongs to

_____

If You Give a Mouse a Cookie

If You Give a

Mouse a Cookie

WRITTEN BY **Laura Numeroff**

ILLUSTRATED BY **Felicia Bond**

A Laura Geringer Book

An Imprint of HarperCollinsPublishers

For Florence & William Numeroff,
the two best parents anyone could
ever possibly want! — L.J.N.

For Stephen — F.B.

If You Give a Mouse a Cookie 25th Anniversary Edition
Text copyright © 1985, 2010 by Laura Joffe Numeroff
Illustrations copyright © 1985, 2010 by Felicia Bond
All rights reserved. Manufactured in Heshan City, China.
No part of this book may be used or reproduced in any manner whatsoever without
written permission except in the case of brief quotations embodied in critical
articles and reviews. For information address HarperCollins Children's Books, a
division of HarperCollins Publishers, 195 Broadway, New York, NY 10007.
www.mousecookiebooks.com
Library of Congress Cataloging-in-Publication Data
Numeroff, Laura Joffe.
    If you give a mouse a cookie.
    Summary: Relating the cycle of requests a mouse is likely to make after you
give him a cookie takes the reader through a young boy's day.
Children's stories, American. [1. Mice — Fiction]
I. Bond, Felicia, ill.   II. Title.
PZ7.N964If   1985   [E]   84-48343
ISBN 978-0-06-212867-6
CIP   AC
20 LEO 10 9

If you give a mouse a cookie,

he's going to ask for a glass of milk.

When you give him the milk,

he'll probably ask you for a straw.

When he's finished, he'll ask for a napkin.

Then he'll want to look in a mirror
to make sure he doesn't
have a milk mustache.

When he looks into the mirror,

he might notice his hair needs a trim.

So he'll probably ask
for a pair of nail scissors.

When he's finished giving himself a trim,
he'll want a broom to sweep up.

He'll start sweeping.

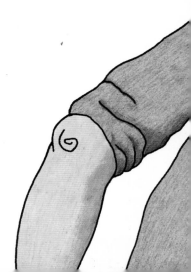

He might get carried away and
sweep every room in the house.

He may even end up washing the floors as well!

When he's done,
        he'll probably want to take a nap.

You'll have to fix up a little box for him
with a blanket and a pillow.

He'll crawl in,
make himself comfortable
and fluff the pillow a few times.

He'll probably ask you to read him a story.

So you'll read to him from one of your books,
and he'll ask to see the pictures.

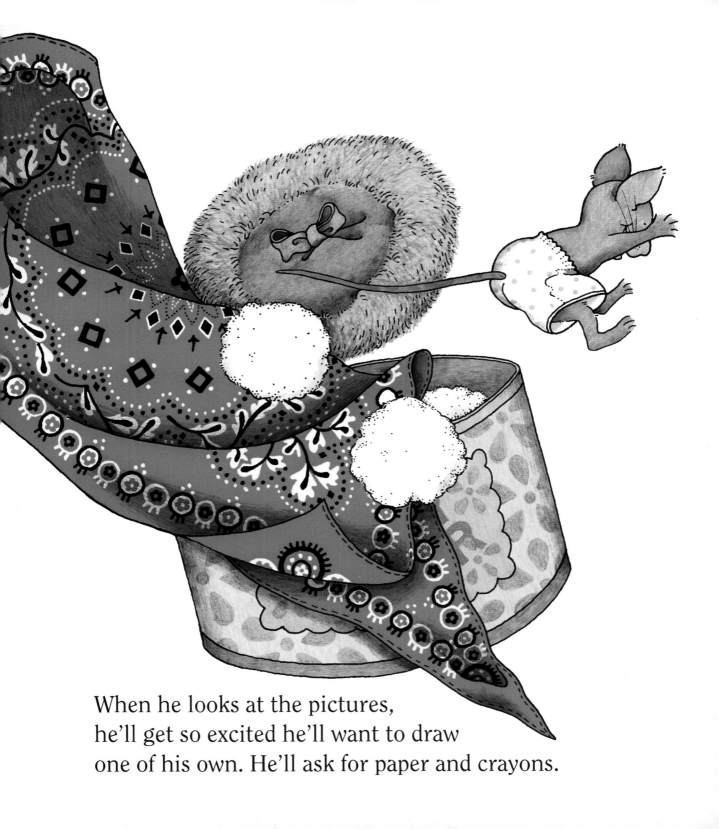

When he looks at the pictures,
he'll get so excited he'll want to draw
one of his own. He'll ask for paper and crayons.

He'll draw a picture.

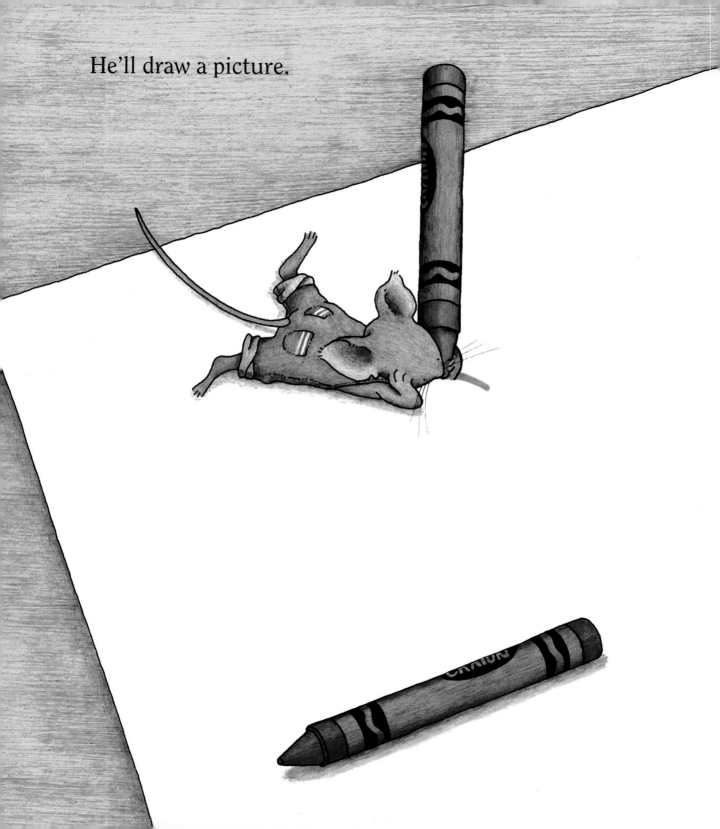

When the picture is finished,

he'll want to sign his name

with a pen.

Then he'll want to hang his picture on your refrigerator.

Which means he'll need

Scotch tape.

He'll hang up his drawing and stand back to look at it.

Looking at the refrigerator will remind him that

he's thirsty.

So . . .

he'll ask for a glass of milk.

And chances are if he asks for
a glass of milk,

he's going to want a cookie to go with it.

START

You need a straw! Move ahead 2!

Hang picture on fridge. Move ahead 1!

Stuck in tape! Lose a turn.

Forgot to sign the picture! Move back 2.

Great picture! Move ahead 2!

Spin again!

The Great Cookie Chase

Borrow a spinner from one of your other board games and create a game piece by coloring and folding a strip of paper. Then take turns moving around the board.

The first one to make it to the end wins the cookies!